Cat, What Is That?

TONY JOHNSTON · PAINTINGS BY WENDELL MINOR

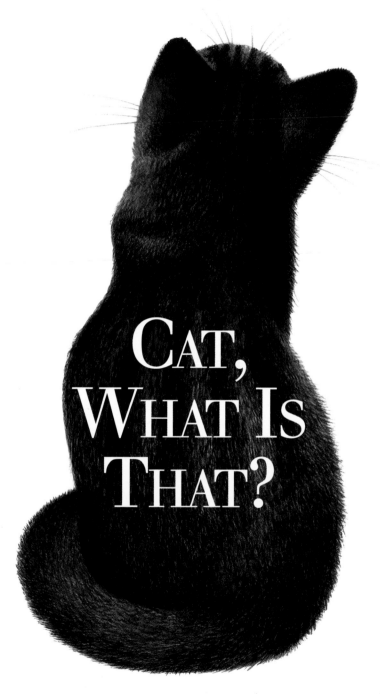

CAT, WHAT IS THAT?

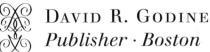

DAVID R. GODINE
Publisher · Boston

It is the Stretch.

It is the Yawn

when a new sun

walks on the lawn.

It is the Rough.

It is the Silk.

It is the *Go-*

get-me-my-milk.

It is the Peek.

It is the Poke.

It is the Dance

on feet of smoke.

Belly down low,

flat to the couch,

buttons, beware!

It is the Crouch.

Up on the sill,

smiling, it thinks.

It is the Know.

It is the Sphinx.

It is the Frisk.

It is the Loon

leaping beneath

a whisker-moon.

It is the Bath
swimming in sun.
It is the Slurp.
It is the Tongue.

It is the Spy
licking its chin
waiting all day,
watching the Fin.

It is the Claw.

It is the Hook.

It is the *Now-*

how-do-I-look?

It is the Pounce.

It is the Roar.

In a snowstorm

it is the Snore.

Rain pounds the roof

with silver nails.

Outside it cries—

Poor Prince of Wails.

It is the Fat,

round as a jar.

It is the Thin,

home from the war.

Its name is Scheme.

Its name is Sly.

Or Celery.

Or Tom-One-Eye.

It is the Curl-

up-in-your-lap.

At any time

it is the Nap.

It is the Slink.

It is the Sneak

on velvet toes

stalking the Squeak.

Here and then gone,

it is the Wink

in summer grass.

Green firefly-blink.

It is the Ghost

haunting the dump.

It is the orange

marmalade Lump.

It is the Wise.

It is the Foof.

Now it is here.

Now it is *poof!*

It is the Hiss.

It is the Howl

when it is nosed

by Mister Jowl.

(A change of mood

can alter this.

Then it is Croon.

Then it is Kiss.)

It is the Hope.

It is the Eyes

lit with green fire,

after the prize.

It is the old

Weaver of string.

Beneath the stars

it is the Sing.

It is the Thief

beside the cream.

Beside the fire

it is the Dream.

For Blacky, Schmoey, and Sugarfoot

–T.J.

For Willie and Sofie, and in memory of Mr. Moe, Miss Kitty, and Mouse

–W.M.

Published in 2008 by
DAVID R. GODINE · *Publisher*
Post Office Box 450
Jaffrey, New Hampshire 03452
www.godine.com

Typography by Wendell Minor and Al Cetta

First softcover printing 2008
Printed in China